Rocket Says Look Up!

Written by
Nathan Bryon

Illustrated by
Dapo Adeola

RANDOM HOUSE NEW YORK

To my favorite stars in the universe—
Mum, Dad, Bro, and my supernova, Theresa —N.B.

Dedicated with love to my five nieces,
especially Sarah, the inspiration behind Rocket.
May you all be forever curious about
the wonders of the world. —D.A.

 Published in the United States by Random House Children's Books, a division of Penguin Random House LLC, New York. Originally published by Puffin Books, an imprint of Penguin Random House Children's Books U.K., a division of Penguin Random House U.K., London, in 2019.

Random House and the colophon are registered trademarks of Penguin Random House LLC.

Visit us on the Web! rhcbooks.com

Educators and librarians, for a variety of teaching tools, visit us at RHTeachersLibrarians.com

Library of Congress Cataloging-in-Publication Data is available upon request.
ISBN 978-1-9848-9442-7 (trade) — ISBN 978-1-9848-9443-4 (ebook)

MANUFACTURED IN CHINA
10 9 8 7 6 5 4 3 2 1
First American Edition

Random House Children's Books supports the First Amendment and celebrates the right to read.

Every night before bed,
I set up my telescope
and wish upon a star. . . .

Mom tells me that I never stop looking up and my head is always floating *in the* clouds.

But she can't tell me that I **LOOK UP** more than my big brother, Jamal, **LOOKS DOWN** at his silly phone.

Jamal says I'm called Rocket because I've got fiery breath.
But Mom says it's because a famous rocket blasted off into space the day I was born!

All I know is that one day I'm going to be the greatest **astronaut, star catcher, space walker** who has ever lived—like Mae Jemison, the first African American woman in space.

DID YOU KNOW . . .
Mae Jemison went into orbit around Earth in the space shuttle *Endeavour*, even though she is afraid of heights?

I'm totally prepared.

I've . . . defied gravity . . .

captured rare and
exotic life-forms . . .

and built a ship to the stars!

For today's mission, I'm going to see something incredible:

THE PHOENIX METEOR SHOWER!

I want **everyone** to see it with me, so I've made some flyers to hand out!

Jamal is going to take me to the park to see the meteor shower. But first we have to go to the supermarket. While he is looking for the milk, I will be trying to find the astronaut food!

DID YOU KNOW . . .
. . . meteor showers happen when Earth moves through the trail of dust left by a comet?
CHAR'S
CAFE

DID YOU KNOW . . .
most meteors are smaller
than a grain of sand?

DID YOU KNOW . . .
meteors are bits of
dust burning up in
the atmosphere?

DID YOU KNOW . . .
the best time to see a
meteor shower is when it's
dark, with no clouds?

In the supermarket, when
Cathy the cashier isn't looking,
I grab the microphone. . . .

And everyone

LOOKS UP!

Cathy takes her microphone back as I hand out my flyers to the other people in the line.

I think Jamal might be a tiny bit annoyed with me.

THE
PHOENIX METEOR SHOWER
will be coming soon—
we'd better drop off the
shopping and get to
the park fast!
"LOOK OUT!"

"Ha ha! That wouldn't have happened if you had just **LOOKED UP!"**

Now Jamal is even more annoyed with me. And he says he won't take me to the park anymore!

But when we get home, Mom saves the day. "Come on, Jamal," she says. "Put the phone down and take your little sister to the park."

YES! I jump up and do my famous victory dance around the room.

I grab my jet-pack backpack,
but Jamal is still glued to his game.

"Wait till I complete this level, Rocket!"
he grumbles.

As we're about to leave, the doorbell rings. . . .

WOW!

It's half the people
from my street,
and they're all
holding my flyers.

"TO THE PARK!"

I yell at the
top of my lungs.
Everyone is
so excited!

My neck is aching from staring up into the night sky, but I won't stop.

I can't miss it!

Suddenly the park goes silent.
Even the birds are holding their breath.

Everyone points their telescopes
and binoculars up at the sky.

Everyone BUT Jamal, who is
STILL LOOKING DOWN
at his phone.

"I THINK I SEE IT!" I shout.

But it's just a plane
flying overhead.
Everyone moans
and groans.

We wait
and wait
and WAIT.

One by one, people start
to leave. . . .

Maybe the Phoenix Meteor Shower was a myth, after all.

Maybe that's why Jamal didn't want to come along.

Maybe everyone is upset with me for wasting their time.

I've never, ever felt
this sad before.

Jamal looks at me for the first time today. It feels like the first time ever.

"I've turned my phone off, sis," he says.

"I'm sorry for making you wait for nothing, Jamal. Let's go home."

Suddenly. . . there's a big bright light in the sky!

Look

UP!!!

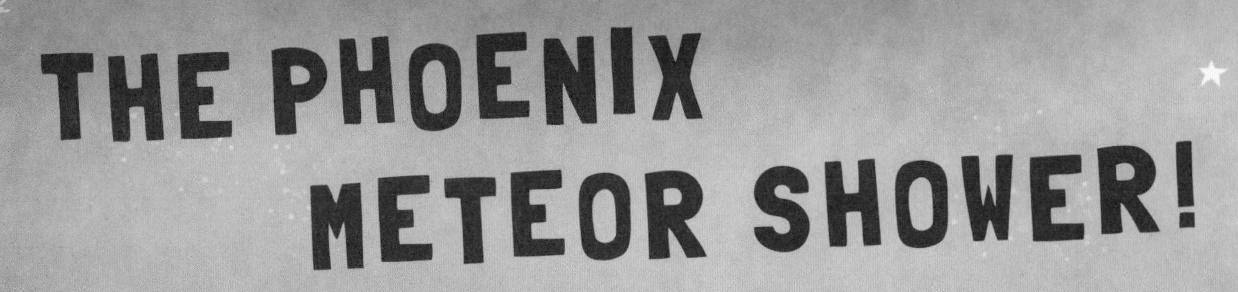

THE PHOENIX METEOR SHOWER!

"I'm speechless," Jamal says. He pulls out his thermos and pours me a cup of hot chocolate. Yummy!

We both sit down on the hill, watching meteors
zoom across the sky.

I'm so happy we

LOOKED UP

and saw them together.